Praise for *Mommy Goose's Appalachian Melodies*

"I opened *Mommy Goose's Appalachian Melodies* out of curiosity, intending to browse, and ended up reading every word, appreciating every picture. This is a book full of fine storytelling, colorful characters, lively wordplay, good sense, and pure fun. The book takes the reader on a delightful journey, all accompanied by Minnie Adkins's whimsical, colorful carvings. *Appalachian Melodies* is an American and Appalachian original."

—Gurney Norman, author of *Allegiance: Stories*
and member of the Kentucky Writers Hall of Fame

"*Appalachian Melodies* is the latest of several collaborations Mike and Minnie have done. Rather than being a mere 'addition' to the series, this work expands and deepens the reach of previous efforts, making the case—without preaching—that all life is local, if it is to be richly lived. We belong to each other—there's no 'us' and 'them.' Here is a lovely and enchanting book that children and parents will want in their homes, their schools, and their local libraries."

—Maurice Manning, author of *Snakedoctor*
and finalist for the Pulitzer Prize for Poetry

"Norris's words are as satisfying, salty, and sweet as that kettle corn we got at the craft fair last October, and Adkins's carvings charm the bark off the tree. *Appalachian Melodies* is homegrown enchantment. Run and buy it. It drips with delight."

—Robert Gipe, author of *Pop: An Illustrated Novel*
and winner of the Weatherford Award for Appalachian Fiction

"*Appalachian Melodies* sings! Minnie Adkins's carvings dance! Another gem in the series—keep 'em coming!"

—T. Crunk, poet, children's book author, and winner of the
Yale Younger Poets Prize for *Living in the Resurrection*

"Bright, original, alive / a book in which to dive — *Appalachian Melodies* delights / children and adults alike."
—Katerina Stoykova, author of *Between a Bird Cage and a Bird House*

"Rhyme has long been out of fashion in both poetry and children's books. And wood carving, a traditional art form, is no longer widely practiced. Fortunately for us, both Norris and Adkins have had the courage to follow their own instincts and talents and to stay at their art and craft over the long haul. The work of these two mature and practiced Kentucky artists culminates beautifully in *Appalachian Melodies*. Readers and listeners of all ages will find so much to delight in here that they may not notice how much they are learning about language and about life."
—Anne Shelby, author of *The Adventures of Molly Whuppie and Other Appalachian Folktales*

Mommy Goose's Appalachian Melodies

Mommy Goose's **APPALACHIAN MELODIES**

MIKE NORRIS ❧ CARVED ILLUSTRATIONS BY MINNIE ADKINS

Publication of this volume was made possible in part by support from the Dan and Merrie Boone Foundation.

Copyright © 2024 by The University Press of Kentucky

Scholarly publisher for the Commonwealth, serving Bellarmine University, Berea College, Centre College of Kentucky, Eastern Kentucky University, The Filson Historical Society, Georgetown College, Kentucky Historical Society, Kentucky State University, Morehead State University, Murray State University, Northern Kentucky University, Spalding University, Transylvania University, University of Kentucky, University of Louisville, University of Pikeville, and Western Kentucky University. All rights reserved.

Editorial and Sales Offices: The University Press of Kentucky
663 South Limestone Street, Lexington, Kentucky 40508-4008
www.kentuckypress.com

Cataloging-in-Publication data available from the Library of Congress

ISBN 978-1-9859-0115-5 (hardcover)
ISBN 978-1-9859-0116-2 (pdf)

This book is printed on acid-free paper meeting
the requirements of the American National Standard
for Permanence in Paper for Printed Library Materials.

Manufactured in Canada.

To Carmen, Cari, John, Samuel, Noemi, Granta Martin, Mother, Granny Norris, Charlie Norris, Jack Norris, Twila Davis, Brenda Harding, and Jess Wilson
—Mike Norris

To my great-grandchildren: twins Lake and Madi Adkins; Lia Adkins; Connor Moore and Emily Moore; Rylan Garner, Melody Garner, and Savana Garner; and Lucas Smith and Cody Smith
—Minnie Adkins

Special thanks to Greg Adkins, Mike Adkins, Margaret Day Allen, Dana Bart, Sharon Boggs, Carmel Bowman, Jeff Bradford, Mark Brown, Jane Collett, Bob Gottlieb, Marlene Grissom, Maggie Hettinger, Ron Hurst, Joyce Ice, Gene Johnson, Sue Keeton, Cathy Lowe, Pam Meade, Loel Meckel, Bill Medl, Jeff Parker, Margaret Rader, Carol Sue Ray, Jim Roach, Noemi Rodriguez, Kate Savage, Frances Shepard, Leslie Smith, Tammy Stone, Bill Sutton, and Vela Walter

Contents

About Mommy Goose, 2

Ingredients, 3
Sally Ann's Reply, 4
The Goat, 5
The Question, 6
The Tools We Have, 6
The Parting, 7
Hoop and Shelf, 8
Remedy, 9
To Lay or Lie, 10
When Tommy Stole Cookies, 10
Ned at the Dance, 11
What Can...?, 12

Sleeping Mistakes, 12
Waltzing with Elephant, 13
Verse and Chorus, 14
What Blind Sam Saw, 15

EXTRA EGGS
The Scribbler, 16
Brother Boyd, 16
Habits, 17
Where Animals Rule, 18
There Was a Large Man, 20
Us and Them, 21

Mrs. Sizemore Says
Don't leaf in a fever
Mommy's rhymes inside.
The fudge can cover
Where the walnuts hide.

Guard at the Gate, 22
Late and Early, 23
The Directions, 23
The Old Woman, 24
Run, Fox, Run, 25
Methuselah Thacker, 26
Smart People, 26
The Moon-Eyed Man, 27
Today, 28
Doc Hale, 28
Granpaw's Nerve Pill, 29

GOOSE TALES
Roadside Zoo, 30
Rabbit and Hound, 32
Soup Bean Soup, 34
The Duck's Predicament, 36
The Cardinal and the Jay, 39
Slow, Quick, and Sly, 41
The Clock that Tocked, 44
Always Remember, 48
Between the Banks, 49
The Promise, 49

"Waltzing with Elephant," *words and music by Mike Norris*, 50

About the Author and Illustrator, 52

Who *redeemed old with kind,*
What *Sam saw though he was blind,*
When *the creatures drew a line,*
Where *Doc went because of crime,*
Why *Sol tied the box with twine,*
And how *two danced in three-four time,*
Tell me, Mommy Goose.

Time is contagious, and we've all caught it.
—*M. Poule*

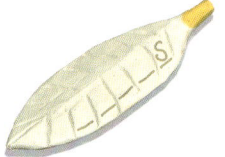

About Mommy Goose

Mommy Goose is partial to books,
And she's way older than she looks.
She writes for food and for fun,
And always claims the place she's from.
Some friends asked the other day,
"What if they gave your words away?"
She said the rhymes were work and play,
But lacking any other way,
She'd write them if she had to pay.

Mommy at work

Though a goose can doze on her feet,
Many a rhyme has ruined my sleep—
But if my rest with verse is strewn,
That's the way you want it ruined.

—M.G.

Ingredients

Bloom dust loads the honeybee's legs.
The cow eats hay and gives some milk.
The hen pecks corn and lays two eggs.
The worm chews leaves and spins out silk.
The crow rolls words across its tongue,
But never will say the food they're from.

Sally Ann's Reply

"Sally Ann, Sally Ann, give me a kiss.
Close your eyes. Lean in like this."

"If I lean, Willie, I'll lean away.
Your breath smells of carbide,
Your hair looks like hay,
And you've not seen soap
In many a day.
Willie, oh, Willie, I tell you true,
I'd court a possum before I'd kiss you."

The Goat

He started to butt when he got his horns.
He butted the kudzu; he butted the corn.
He butted the kitten; he butted the hen.
He butted the boards around the pig's pen.
He butted the dog; he butted the calf.
He butted the pitchfork and broke it in half.
He butted the sheep and tore out some wool.
The last one he butted was Daddy's bull.

The Question

It's been four days.
You're filled with doubt.
Heat it up? Throw it out?

Hold it close.
Sniff it well.
Uumm, or uuhh, the smell will tell.

The Tools we have are Twenty-Six.
Good or Bad is all in The mix.
You can choose for Pain or Pleasure.
Use The leTTeRS To make Things BeTTeR.

The Parting

He stands and grieves
   before the glass.
What little's left
   is going fast,
And with the loss
   each racing year,
The part creeps closer
   to his ear.
He lifts his arm
   into position,
And rolls the comb
   with sly precision:
Up and over,
   now down the far side,
So little to cover,
   so much to hide.
He spreads it thin
   across the scalp,
Smears to close
   a tiny gap,
Gives one stray strand
   a final tap,
Then goes to get
   his baseball cap.

Hoop and Shelf

Biddledy boop on a quilting hoop,
If you've got ice cream,
Give me a scoop.

Riddledy relf on a whatnot shelf,
If you've got the flu,
Keep to yourself.

Remedy

Putting off will make it worse.
To feel better faster,
Do the hard thing first.

To Lay or Lie

On lay and lie,
Lest you forget,
Lie is recline,
Lay is to set.

Though odd, the past
Of lie is lay,
But we'll save that
For another day.

Last, to lie earns
A nose that grows.
This you learned
Long ago.

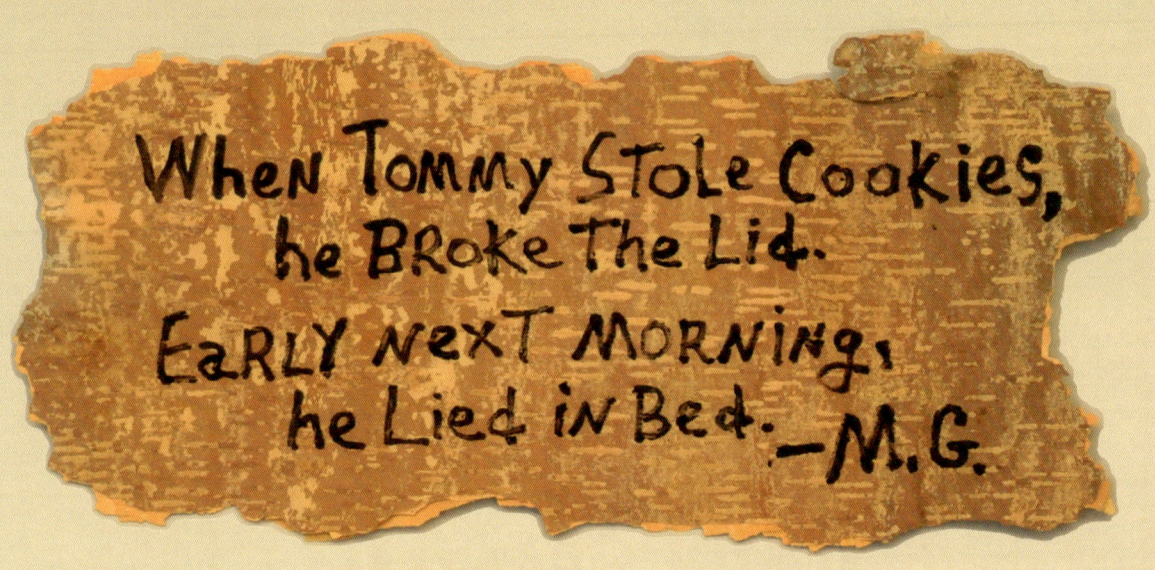

When Tommy stole cookies, he broke the lid.
Early next morning, he lied in bed. —M.G.

Ned at the Dance

Ned was twenty and wanted a bride,
So he went to the frolic to give it a try.
The last thing Ned could do was dance,
But he hit the floor and took a chance.
Two young women sat on the side.
"Bad dancing," one whispered, "stabs my eyes.
And him without sense enough to quit.
It looks more like he's having a fit."
The other watched, nursing her chin:
"I've been gauging all these men.
The others can dance; that one can't,
But he's the very one I want."
Her friend's eyes swelled, then her voice:
"Surely you'd not make such a choice!"
The other patted in time to the song:
"You study short. I study long.
Sometimes it's this for that in a trade.
He may not can dance, but he's not afraid."
And those were the terms of the bargain she made.

Because Ned dared, they raised five sons.
All did well, but dancers? Not one.

What Can…?
Make them laugh,
Make them cry,
Snatch a breath,
And say, "Oh, my!"

Sleeping Mistakes
Late to bed, early to rise,
Yawn all day, rub your eyes.

Early to bed, late to rise,
Carry a fan, shoo off flies.

Waltzing with Elephant

Elephant dreamily,
Dancing me awkwardly,
Pulling me next to his
Very long nose.

This could be serious,
Possibly dangerous.
Praying he never does
Step on my toes.

Two-ton calamity,
Stomping out *one*-two-three.
Song's like a century,
Still on it goes.

Hoping he'll take a break
Soon to recuperate.
Why did I stay so late?
Lord only knows.

Waltz of eternity, dragging on endlessly,
Finally…mercifully, comes to a close.

Elephant bows to me, thanks me with courtesy.
Then out of nowhere he…hands me a rose.

Quite unexpectedly, seeing it differently,
New possibilities, now I suppose.

Verse and Chorus

Mommy cut up cabbage,
And seasoned it with salt.
I said I was hungry,
And she gave me the stalk.

*"Well, well, stay awhile.
We're all kin, you know."
"If you grieve, we won't leave
For home until we go."*

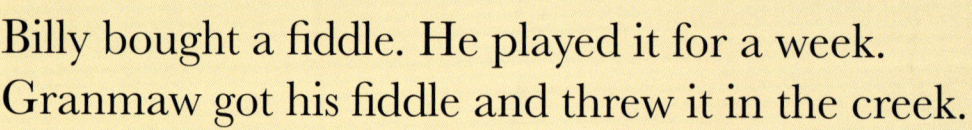

Billy bought a fiddle. He played it for a week.
Granmaw got his fiddle and threw it in the creek.

*Boo, hoo, what'll we do about the stormy weather?
Wrap some yarn around the barn and huddle up together.*

Granpaw took the toothache. It kept him up all night.
He hit it with a hammer because he wasn't right.

*Oh, my, who'll try to tell the tallest tale?
"Lester Frye was born to lie. Too bad he's still in jail."*

Sunday when we visit, don't stare at Uncle Lou.
Someday if you're lucky, you'll look that way too.

*Ho, hey, who can say where time has gone so fast?
Drive the car away from there until it's out of gas.*

What Blind Sam Saw

I dreamed it was winter and I could see
That words were snowing down on me.
Turned to the moon, I held out my hand
And touched each one as it would land.
They fell with sense and inward sound,
And with each step, I read the ground.
The lines laid out in artful time,
A blend of near and perfect rhyme.
I willed this scene to never end,
And yearn each night to dream again.
Visions come as they will choose,
And now this wondrous door is closed,
But though awake, I walk that ground,
To see the way the words come down.

EXTRA EGGS

*Raiding the henhouse, all in a rush,
It's easy to miss a hidden stash.
Reach a little deeper down in the hay,
And you might find the egg of the day.*
—M.G.

The Scribbler
The weight of words,
You have to bear it.
Befriend your idea,
Never marry it.

Brother Boyd
As time tattoos what you love most,
Look in the mirror, but not too close.

Habits

Shirk the work, wear out the couch,
Strow your clothes over the house.
Leave the dishes in the sink,
Spend it all before you think.
Shade the truth to reach your ends,
Say bad things about your friends.

Brush your teeth, wash your hands,
Scrub the dirty pots and pans.
Bend your back, bear the load,
Pay each person what is owed.
Rule your temper when it swells,
Take the time to listen well.

Habits tick and habits tock,
Through the daily take and give.
Some make sand, some make rock.
They are most of how we live.

Where Animals Rule

"People!" neighed the horse. "Can't abide 'em.
Even with a saddle, you can't ride 'em."
The chicken chimed in, "They're the dregs.
You'll never see one lay an egg."
The cat sat down and licked her paw:
"Pathetic!" she mewed. "Can't even claw."
All at once the hog spoke up:
"And they think they're too good for slop."

The animals had gathered beneath a pine,
To sniff the problem and draw a line.

A bear pointed to his purple pants:
"Train us for tricks and make us dance.
Strap on a chain, pull us and jerk us,
Make us act foolish, and call it a circus."
"A circus?" growled the tiger. "That sorry bunch!
If one tried to train me, I'd eat it for lunch."

The animals rose up and began to squall,
"Down with people. Down with 'em all."

Just then an owl lit on a limb:
"For sure," he hooted, "us or them.
They've got to be the world's worst creatures,
With hurtful ways and foolish features.
Gobs go hungry, starving to death,
As the big ones eat till they can't draw breath.
When it's time to work, some just rest,
While others toil themselves to death.
And if one might get the gift to grow old,
Call it that and its blood runs cold.
But here's the thing way worse than the rest—
As a flock they're dirty and foul the nest."

"Agreed!" screamed a crow. "Downright evil.
Something's got to be done about people!"

"Well now," said the owl, "it's clear the case,
But that agreed, let's not act in haste.
Humans are plainly harm and vexation,
Still yet, they're part of nature's creation.
We needn't start with a lot of bother.
More likely than not, they'll end one another.
So mercy can guide our governing role
To treat people kindly (though under control).
We can set some traps, round up the last few,
Keep them in cages, and call it a zoo."

"Vote now!" roared the bear, raising a paw,
"So it'll be legal, according to law.
Then *they* can do tricks and sleep on straw."

The crows broke out in a chorus of caws,
And the plan was approved with wild applause.

There Was a Large Man

There was a large man,
   unbuckled his belt,
Hey, ho, over the waves.
The more he ate,
   the worse he felt,
Rum, dum, down in the caves.

He filled his bowl
   beyond the brim,
Bar, dar, splashes and spills.
He bit his bread,
   his bread bit him.
Flim, flum, fevers and chills.

They laid him by
   the churchyard gate,
Bim, bam, under the clover.
Now he can't taste,
   early or late,
Lo, wo, the potluck supper.

Us and Them

We are us and they are them,
And she is her and he is him.
I am me and you are you,
And they can be no less than two.
But what if with some magic trick,
Us and them would make a switch,
And we could learn to not forget,
The them is us we haven't met?
Then all the we might come to trust
That there's no them but only us.

Guard at the Gate

A man was hired to be town guard.
"None," they said, "unclean are allowed."
After an hour denying every guest,
He questioned, and then answered himself:
"Because all are dirty, each one who passes,"
But later discovered it was only his glasses.

Late and Early

When the wintery king extends his reign,
We sit inside, yawn, and complain,
While the robins are about the business of spring.

The Directions

Dry clean only,
Avoid baloney.
Coffee is hot,
Unless it's not.
Holler below,
Mountains above,
Handle with care,
Do not remove.
Objects are closer
Than they appear.
(It's way too late
When they seem near.)

The Old Woman

How high is high?
How low is low?
How fast is fast?
How slow is slow?

The sky is high.
The sea is low.
Time is fast.
It once was slow.

Run, Fox, Run

Hear the hounds' music. It's about to begin.
Run, fox, run, away from the den.
All summer in cages, craving their fun,
The hounds are leaping. Run, fox, run.

Already they're tracing your zigzag trail.
Reading the leaves, they taste your smell.
Through the creek and still they come.
The hounds are gaining. Run, fox, run.

On and on with every trick,
Along the fence, then double back.
Stop and rest, the race is done.
The hounds keep coming. Run, fox, run.

One last chance before you break,
Into the swamp, over the snakes.
Hounds follow close, noses down,
Then all at once, a fearful sound.

Up the hill and down the far side,
The hounds have scattered, broken stride.
On through darkness till you see sun,
The hounds arc waiting. Run, fox, run.

Methuselah Thacker

It's not much fun,
To be a hundred and one.

Smart People

It's amazing how clever others can be,
Expressing views with which we agree.

The Moon-Eyed Man

One day walking Four-twenty-one,
I came upon a moon-eyed man.
His eyes so wide and skin so white,
He asked if he was headed right.
I declared I didn't know,
And asked him where he wanted to go.
His eyes lit up and he grinned at me:
"Why, son, the courthouse in McKee.
Got business there, I recollect,
Pledge to pay, debt to collect."
I pointed west and nodded him on.
Out the road stretched, straight and long,
But when I looked back, he was gone.

They had a big trial in town that day.
The judge took sick and was carried away.
The moon that night turned deathly white,
And the judge went on before first light.
They buried him by a hemlock tree,
Court was adjourned, the prisoner went free.
When he turned to shade his face with his hand,
It put me in mind of the moon-eyed man.

Today

Some days bring trouble.
Some days bring friends.
The bad and the good,
They have an end.
This day will never
Come again.

Doc Hale

Old Doc Hale broke the rule,
And went to Atlanta, but not for school.
When he came back, he changed his name,
But doctored people just the same.
Now he's gone, they don't agree
About his old-time remedies.
Some say good, some say bad,
But he was here and all we had.

Granpaw's Nerve Pill

When I was young, I'd leap from bed.
But up in age, I creak instead.
Time is paid as the debt comes due.
And a high-priced lawyer can't talk you new,
Even if he decides to sue.
The doctor can't make a young old man,
Even with a three-part treatment plan.
The preacher can't pray the years away,
Even if he prays all day.
But here's a thing that commonly helps—
Do a kindness for someone else.
There comes a feeling of gladsome calm,
Once the helping thing is done.
You may look stiff and ugly and old,
But the deed you did is good to behold.

GOOSE TALES

*In gosling days, I was in my glory,
When Granny would say, "Let me tell you a story."*
—M.G.

Roadside Zoo

Among the attractions at a roadside zoo
Were a mountain lion and a kangaroo.
They stayed apart and mostly kept quiet,
Till the lion whispered, "I'd win in a fight."

The roo's ears stood; he said to his neighbor:
"Those bars between do you a big favor.
You could take a rabbit and maybe a deer,
But you best be glad you're not over here."
"I'm surprised," said the lion, "at talk like that,
Coming from a stub-armed, overgrown rat.
I'd cover the ground in just one leap,
And give you a taste of claws and teeth."
The roo hopped nearer the lion's cage:
"Those teeth make plain you're up in age.
If you jumped me, you crouching sneak,
I'd boot you all the way to next week."
The lion snarled and began to roar.
The roo bent back, kicking the air.

Just then a gnat flew in between.
"Whoa, boys," she yelled, "talking mean,
Making claims of what you'd do,
And hear how I've got it over you."
The lion hushed, he was so dumbstruck.
The roo came down and straightened up.

Lit on a can, the gnat cleared her throat:
"Now, y'all may be big, but I gnaw on you both.
And you think you're fast, but to me you're slow,
And bide behind bars while I come and go.
So, dusty jailbirds that can't even fly,
Brief as it's been, I'll say goodbye.
I'm off to drink from an elephant's eye."

The lion yawned; the roo licked an arm,
And hopped to a spot in the afternoon sun.
They kept a cool distance after that,
But agreed to never speak of the gnat.

Rabbit and Hound

A hound and a rabbit got in a race.
One ran to live, the other to taste.
The rabbit was quick, zigging and zagging,
But before too long, her strength was lagging.
The hound was strong, his legs were long,
And pounding the ground, he kept coming on.
The rabbit drew deep, called on her will,
And raced to the cliff up Mountain Hill.
Hound came bounding, rabbit stopped,
And the hound went sliding over the top.
He clawed a bush, clung with one paw,
As to and fro he swung in the air.
"Help!" he squalled. "I'll die if I drop."
The rabbit honked, and off she hopped.
"I know," yelled the hound, "you're mad at me.
But we go way back. I knew your daddy.
Not only him, but Sue before that,
And where they all lived on Chestnut Flat."
The rabbit turned. "You knew Aunt Sue?"
"I did," said the hound, "and you favor her too.
Help me up for the sake of old friends,
And I pledge never to chase you again."

As the rabbit considered how she'd been treated,
The bush slipped, and the hound pleaded,
"Come to the edge and let your tail drop.
I'll grab hold and pull to the top."
The rabbit inched closer and twitched her nose:
"That might do if that's how it goes,
But hounds tell tales is what I heard.
How do I know you'll keep your word?"
The bush slipped again; the hound howled despair:
"No chasing never, *forever*, I swear."
The rabbit's ears wavered; then slowly she turned
And backed to the edge while the hound squirmed.
She lowered her tail near the dog's lips;
He took hold and clawed his way up.
But the tail was fat; he smelled rabbit flavor,
And bit off a little piece of his neighbor.
"Ayeeee," she screamed, leaping away,
"Save your life, and here's my pay!"
The hound wiped scraps of fur from a tooth:
"Word for word, you heard the truth.
I only swore I wouldn't chase.
Never said nothing 'bout taking a taste."
The rabbit's ears bent; she stood to shout,
"You lied like a dog by what you left out!"
Then off she hopped toward Rabbit Town,
Squealing each time her stub hit ground.

Friends ran up when she came off trail,
And stared at what was left of the tail.
She told it all and blamed herself.
Now whenever hounds hurt, rabbits won't help.

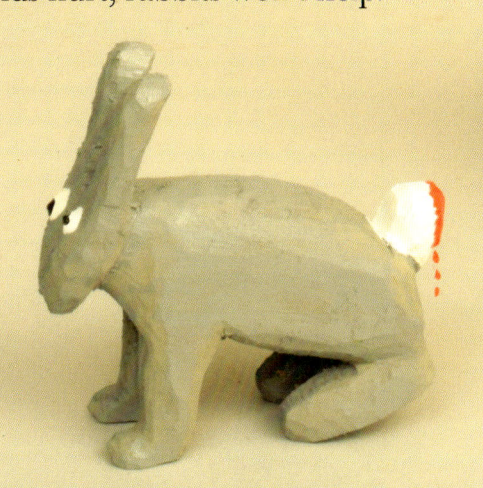

Soup Bean Soup

When spring began to show its face,
Nothing was left but scraps at our place.
Daddy brought in some squirrels and rabbits,
But they got smart and changed their habits.
Mommy said soon there'd be more to eat.
Poke could be picked in another week.
With brother sick and all thin as pine,
A week seemed like a year of time.
The baby kept crying and Mommy said,
"Let's eat what we've got before it goes bad."
Daddy looked off and nodded his head.

She laid it out on the kitchen table:
Half cup of meal and a sweet potato,
A few broke beans from down in the bag,
And some turnip tops, limp as a rag.
She boiled the beans till after dark,
While the cut-up potato baked on the hearth.
Then every last bit went into the pot.
At last, Mommy said, "Now, while it's hot."

She handed Daddy the gravy ladle.
And sat six cups around the table,
He went to the stove, one by one,
And filled them all except his own.
Mommy said, "Will, you can't not eat."
Daddy just smiled. "Resting my teeth."
We got it down, but it wasn't good.
Mommy said, "To cook, you got to have food.
The way it tasted wasn't my fault."
Daddy smiled again. "Needed more salt."

He was up next morning before first light,
And said look for him way in the night.
He left wearing boots, but came back in bare feet
With a bag of beans and a piece of ham meat.
Late as it was, Mommy cooked a meal,
And we all sat and ate our fill.

So long past, but still I think back
To that hungry spring we had in our shack.
It was hard, a sad time, and yet I feel happy
That he was who I had for a daddy.

The Duck's Predicament

We kept a duck that swam in the pond,
Across and back, all day long.
One day a turtle rose from the bottom,
Feet flapped by, and the snapper got one.
The duck disappeared in a sidelong jerk,
And the children cried when he didn't come up.
My woman saw it from beyond the porch,
And made us all go back in the house.
Through the evening, the little ones mourned,
And early next morning I went to the barn.
As I shook the basket to gather eggs,
There stood the duck on just one leg.

He kept to the barn, hopping, then sitting,
In fear, we reckoned, the turtle would get him.
But after four Sundays had come and gone,
There he was, back on the pond.
The children claimed it would be his end,
So I got some scraps and built a pen.
He fared well enough for nigh a week,
But then sulled and barely would eat.
We talked till late, but couldn't agree,
And went to see what Granny would say.
Already in nightclothes, she'd loosed her hair,
And sat by the bed in her rocking chair.
She'd heard it all, for pond or pen,
But back and around we talked it again.
She studied her lap and combed and rocked.
At last, she planted her feet and spoke:
"He may die in water and live boarded up,
And for some that breathe that'd be enough.
But a duck in its nature was made to swim,
So tear down the pen and let him be him."
Then she reached and pulled her sheet:
"Now let a old woman get some sleep."

Right after breakfast, the pen came down,
And the duck half hopped, half flew to the pond.
On he swam and on and on.
With Granny long gone, still he swam on,
Him yet on the pond and the children grown,
And then one of them with a girl of her own.
Full fifteen years he swam in circles,
And time turned out to be his turtle.

38

The Cardinal and the Jay

"Where you going this chilly morning?"
The cardinal said to the jay.
"I'm headed south for the sake of my health,"
I heard the blue bird say.

"I'm surely peeved, to see you leave,
As springtime breaks a grin.
I thought we'd see what summer brought,
And visit now and again."

"I've had enough where winter's rough,
And water tastes of sulfur.
Fighting squirrels and dread of owls
Has given me an ulcer."

"Well, then, the patch you all would peck,
That never left you hungry,
Would be fair game for us to claim,
With you in another country."

"Why, no," said the jay, hopping away.
"I'd shun that soggy ground.
Likely as not, the acorns'll rot
Well before they're found."

"But there's no harm, since you'll be gone,
To save us all some time.
Though the nest she piled is not our style,
The sticks'll serve just fine."

"I'd spare the nest and all the rest
In our old hickory tree.
Its twigs are sharp, and moldy bark
Was nigh the death of me."

"I never said—it slipped my mind,
Who's come without a warning.
The little jay hen is back again.
We spoke just yesterday morning."

"Is that sure true? The last I knew
She'd gone to Tennessee.
In all the talk, the time you spoke,
Was there any word of me?"

"No," said the redbird. "Not that I heard.
While she perched above a mob,
The bachelor boys was making noise,
And dancing their springtime bob."

"Of all that come, did ery a one
Charm her to fly away?"
"One jay's call was over them all,
Full of fire and play.

He finally stopped and stared straight up.
'Very fine singing,' she said.
But when that bird begged for a word,
She smiled and shook her head."

The jay looked down, scratched the ground,
Then preened his foremost feathers:
"As days unfold, we'll trade the cold
For blooms and warmer weather.

I feel my blood beginning to run,
And calling me to fly.
On time creeps; words'll keep.
And so I'll say goodbye."

The cardinal squawked, "But we've not talked
Of beetle bugs that's hid.
Forsaking food that's still yet good
Wastes all the work you did."

The jay ignored the redbird's words,
Hinting for a favor.
He took to air away from there,
But called back to his neighbor:

"I'll not leave what's home to me,
For fear of biding alone.
Time to attend a little blue hen,
Before the chance has flown."

Slow, Quick, and Sly

On the road in opposite ways,
The Quick ran by the Slow one day.
Quick came back and studied Slow.
He smiled and said, "You barely go.
To plod along at such a pace,
I'd hang my head and hide my face.
You're like a rock with stumpy legs,
Of all that move, you're sure the dregs."

The Slow then slowly turned her head.
"You're keen to judge and shame," she said.
"Because I'm slow, you think I'm thick,
And right's with you because you're quick.
But taking movement for the deed,
May reach the wrong with greater speed.
I'd like to go with style and grace,
But some weren't made to move in haste."

The Quick then circled round the Slow:
"Such as you were meant for low.
Nature surely shaped you wrong,
The race is to the swift and strong."

Just then the Sly came into sight.
The Quick, his eyes enlarged in fright,
Tore away like he'd done a crime,
While on Slow trudged, step at a time.
When Sly came up, Slow clamped shut.
He bit her back, and broke a tooth.

Then Sly saw Quick out way ahead,
And took toward him with middling speed.
Quick looked back to yell and laugh,
"You'll have to do way more than that."
He raised a paw and threw a kiss:
"Wanta see fast?…Watch this!"
Quick shot away, but Sly only slowed,
And raising eyes on down the road,
Wet his lips and sniffed the wind,
Of his waiting mate around the bend.

The Clock that Tocked

Harlie and Mildred liked things neat.
They polished the plates before they'd eat.
The house clicked along like a windup machine
Till she left to tend her sick Aunt Jean.

Harlie kept busy the day she left,
And enjoyed having the place to himself.
He ate his supper on a shiny plate,
Then had two pieces of cushaw cake.
Late that night, he slipped off to sleep,
But before first light was on his feet.

He took the big-eye the second night,
As the house would creak, then get too quiet.
Setting their clock next to the bed,
He let the rhythm run through his head.
Tick-tock, *tick*-tock slowly brought relief,
And just after four, he sunk into sleep.
He dreamed a big clock was beating a drum,
But after a time, the rhythm went wrong.
With no high beats to balance them out,
Tocks began booming, steady and stout.
When the clock rose up and reached for him,
Harlie tried to yell, but his mouth went numb.
Straining to run away from the hands,
It felt like his feet were plowing sand.
He jerked up in bed, gasping and sweating:
"Just a bad dream I'll soon be forgetting."
But then it seemed like his brain would break.
Tocks were tocking and he was awake.
He got out of bed, switched on the light,
And shook the clock, but it still wasn't right:
"A racket like this'll make a man sick.
It's piling up tocks with nary a tick!"
He gathered the quilts, covered the clock,
And went round the house, checking the locks.
Then back to the bed, he lifted the covers,
But the clock was tocking, louder than ever.
To the trash back and forth he took it all day,
But Mildred didn't like to throw things away.
The next two nights were just the same,
And then without warning, she came.
"Harlie," said Mildred, "the bed's not made.
The dishes are dirty. You've not shaved.
Nothing's been attended to!
What in the world's got in to you?"
He led her by the wrist to a cedar chest,
Opened it up and said, "Listen to this."
"To what?" she said. "It's just the clock ticking."
"No," Harlie yelled. "It's not ticking. It's tocking."
He told the story, and when he was through,
Mildred thought maybe she was hearing it too.
After an hour of walking the floor,
They took it to Sol at the hardware store.

Sol stood at the counter as they walked in,
And over his face fell the shade of a frown.
Harlie told the story and shook his head:
"Stange, odd, unnatural," he said.
"The timepiece is not even nine years old,
But clearly the tocks are out of control."
"You sold it," said Mildred. "Now make it right."
And she braced herself, ready to fight.
Sol studied them both and nodded his head.
"I think I know what's wrong," he said.
"The wheels inside aren't running right,
And something for certain's wound too tight.
Let me go in the back and try a trick.
I don't doubt what's off can be fixed."
He parted the curtain, was back in a minute:
"A unloose screw was knocking in it.
I put it right and oiled the tick guard,
And that cured the problem. No charge."
Mildred looked at Harlie and he at her.
She laid both hands flat on the counter.
"Too fast!" she shouted, lowering her head.
"Nothing for nothing. Sounds just like it did."
Harlie said, "It might be a *little* better,"
But she kept complaining and Harlie let her.
"All right," said Sol, "I can set it straight,
But it's teejus work; you'll have to wait."

Hid behind curtains, Sol stayed a long time,
But finally brought out a box tied with twine.
He opened it up and took out two clocks.
"This ticks," he said. "Your old one just tocks.
Side by side, they balance the sound,
And keep perfect time, long as they're wound.
Detocking a clock is a bunch of trouble,
So here's the ticket charging you double."
Mildred took the bill, then dropped it like lead.
"Yes, I hear it now," she said.

Harlie and Mildred meet each night at nine.
They sit between clocks to share their time,
Harlie reading the paper, Mildred knitting,
One clock, tocking, the other, ticking.
The mood of the room is neatly serene,
And the house clicks along like a windup machine.

WORDS

Always Remember, words are Friends,
That help us weave the outs and ins.
It's good to have a lot of Friends.

Between the banks of they and we,
A river runs called Mystery.
Look up before you guarantee.
A rainbow has colors none can see.

The Promise

Days tick on and still they run,
But after a span, ours are done.
The time with you was full and fine,
Just within hearing of each distant line.
Many a page left the drawer,
And many a shaving hit the floor.
I hope these rhymes have nourished you,
And want you to know, they fed me too.
When flown away to far-off birds,
I'll think of you reading these words.
Take some to heart and some to mind,
And they'll return to you in time,
To rouse a glow like wayward friends,
Whose faces make us young again.

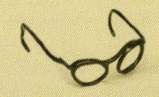

Waltzing with Elephant

Mike Norris
arr. Maggie Hettinger

Capo 3:

1. El-e-phant dream-i-ly dan-cing me awk-ward-ly, pull-ing me next to his ve-ry long nose. This could be ser-i-ous, pos-si-bly dan-ger-ous, pray-ing he ne-ver does step on my toes.

2. Two ton ca-lam-i-ty stomp-ing out 1! 2 3. Song's like a cen-tu-ry, still on it goes. Waltz of e-ter-ni-ty, drag-ging on end-less-ly, fi-nal-ly, mer-ci-fully comes to a close.

3. El-e-phant bows to me, thanks me with cour-te-sy. Then out of no-where, he hands me a rose. Quite un-ex-pect-ed-ly, see-ing it dif-f'rent-ly, new pos-si-bi-li-ties, now, I sup-pose.

(G) B♭ (C) E♭ (F) A♭ (C) E♭ (Dm) Fm (G) B♭
Waltz - ing with E-le-phant. El - e - phant waltz - ing me
(F) A♭ (C) E♭ (Am) Cm (F) A♭ (G) B♭
1.2.
Waltz - ing with El-e- phant How long can this waltz
(C) E♭ (F) A♭ (C) E♭ (F) A♭ (G) B♭ (C) E♭ (Am) Cm
3.
be? Quite un-ex - pec - ted - ly.
(F) A♭ (G) B♭ (C) E♭ (Am) Cm (F) A♭
New pos - si - bi - li - ties of E - le - phant
(G) B♭ (C) E♭ (F) A♭ (Dm) Fm (G7) B♭7 (C) E♭
waltz - ing with me.
ritard

About the Author and Illustrator

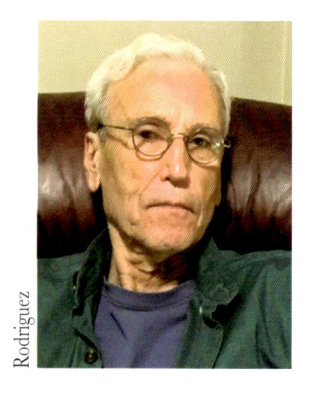

Mike Norris

A native of Eastern Kentucky, Mike Norris writes and has recorded one album with the Raggedy Robin String Band as well as four albums of original music with the Americana group Billyblues. He has published four other children's books: *Sonny the Monkey, Bright Blue Rooster, Mommy Goose: Rhymes from the Mountains*, and *Ring Around the Moon: Mommy Goose Rhymes*. Norris received the 2022 Literary Arts Award from Kentucky organization Arts Connect for poems and stories that "can be read again and again to reveal new levels of meaning and literary artistry." He lives in Lexington with his wife, Carmen.

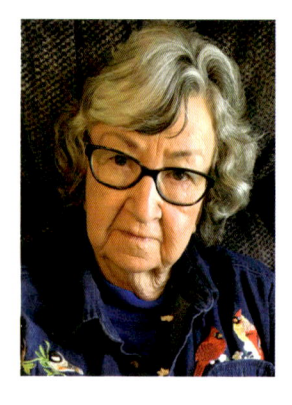

Minnie Adkins

Carving since she was a child, Minnie Adkins is one of America's best-known folk artists. Among many honors, she has won the Folk Art Society of America Distinguished Artist Award, the Governor's Award for the Arts, the Appalachian Treasure Award, and a South Arts Master Artist Fellowship. Her work is part of many permanent collections, including those of the Smithsonian Museum, the National Gallery of Art, Huntington Museum of Art, and the Kentucky Folk Art Center. She has illustrated four other children's books—*Sonny the Monkey, Bright Blue Rooster, Mommy Goose: Rhymes from the Mountains*, and *Ring Around the Moon: Mommy Goose Rhymes*—and lives near her birthplace in Isonville, Kentucky.

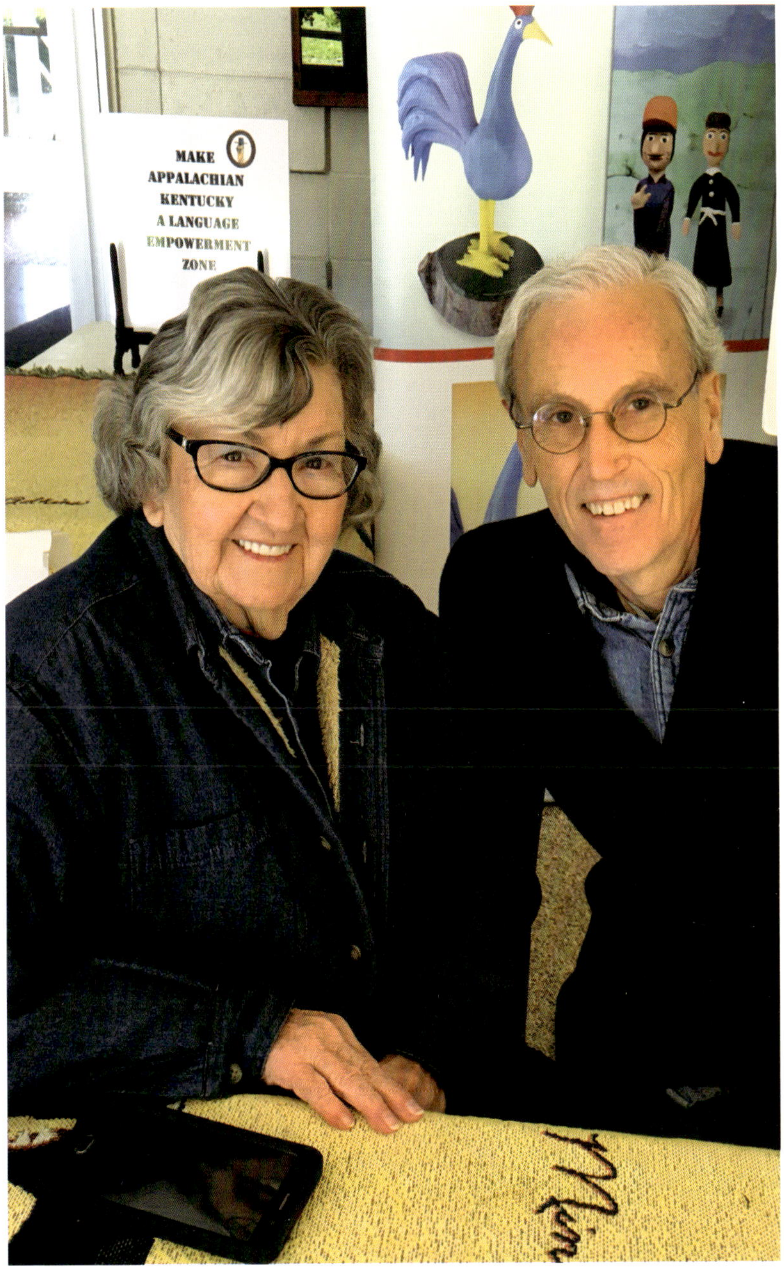
MAKE
APPALACHIAN
KENTUCKY
A LANGUAGE
EMPOWERMENT
ZONE